A Handful of Beans

Six Fairy Tales Retold by **Jeanne Steig** *with Pictures by* **William Steig**

SCHOLASTIC INC.

New York Toronto London Auckland Sydney
Mexico City New Delhi Hong Kong

ISBN 0-439-10132-8

12 11 10 9 8 7 6 5 4 3 2 1   9/9 0 1 2 3 4/0

Printed in the U.S.A.   23

First Scholastic printing, October 1999

Designed by Fred Marcellino

For

Eli, Emma, Ethan, Evan, Itamar, Jake, Katherine Anne, Leor,
Lily, Maia, Peter McGee, Shira, Uri, Tomer

Contents

Rumpelstiltskin

A poor miller went to sell flour to the King, and when he had finished his business, he couldn't resist a bit of bragging. "My daughter," he said, "is more beautiful than all the flowers in Your Majesty's garden."

"Hum, hum," said the King.

"What's more," the miller went on, "she is far more clever than all of Your Majesty's wise men."

"Well, isn't that nice," yawned the King.

"And," said the miller, who couldn't *begin* to control his tongue, "that girl can spin straw into gold."

"Why, the sweet thing! She sounds enchanting," said the King, who was known far and wide for his greed. "Bring her around tomorrow at dawn. I'll give her a little test."

There was nothing the foolish miller could do but deliver his poor daughter up to the King, who wasted no time but led her at once to a huge room full of straw.

"There is your wheel," he told her. "Get busy, my girl. You have till tomorrow morning to spin every blade of this straw into gold."

"That can not be done!" she cried.

But the King said only, "If you fail, you die." And he left her, locking the door behind him. When she was alone, she sat herself down at the wheel, gazed at the mountain of straw, and wept, for her beauty was useless, and her cleverness, too.

All at once the door flew open, and in stomped a bizarre little man with a pickle-shaped nose and a lumpish body. He was just as tall as a sack of grain, and his clothes were outlandish.

"What are you bawling and squalling about?
Some fiddle-dee-diddle, I have no doubt,"

he roared, with a snaggletoothed grin.

"If I don't spin this straw into gold, I must die," she sobbed, "and it can't be done."

"No, it can't be done by you, my dear,
    As any clod can see,
    But give me those beads from around your neck
    And leave the job to me!"

She gave him her beads, and he took his place at the wheel and began to spin. As the wheel raced and the reels filled up with gold, he sang:

"A handful of straw and a whir, whir, whir,
    A thistle, a nettle, a cockleburr.
    Three times round, and the job is done,
    The beads are mine, and the gold is spun!"

The sun hardly had time to raise its head when the King arrived. "My, my," said he, staring at his new gold, "what a lovely surprise. We must do this again." And he led the girl into another room full of straw, much larger than

the first. "I'll see you tomorrow at dawn," he said. *"Spin for your life."*
Again the miller's daughter wept, and again the door flew open.

> "What a terrible snuffle and screak and moo,
> It makes my blood run cold—
> When the one little thing you've been asked to do
> Is turn this straw to gold,"

drawled the odd little person, glancing about with his odd little smile.
"But it can't be done," said she.
The fellow gave her a little pat, and crooned:

> "Well, it can't be done by you, Young Miss,
> Not even to please a king,
> But I'm happy to do the job myself
> For the gift of your pretty ring."

The girl pulled the little ring from her finger and gave it to him, and he sat down at once and began to spin and sing:

"A handful of straw and a whir, whir, whir,
Peppergrass, pigweed, and cockleburr.
Three times round and the job is done,
The ring is mine and the gold is spun!"

The King arrived with the sun's first rays, as happy as a hog with a herring to see the room filled with gold. But his greed only grew with his wealth. He led her into a third room, still larger than the first two, saying, "Spin. If you fail, you die. However, if you succeed, I shall make you my wife." She's only a miller's daughter, thought he, but I must admit she *is* a treasure.

"This time I am surely lost," she said, and sobbed pitifully.

But again the door burst open, and in hopped the strange manikin. He twirled around on one stubby toe, and warbled:

"Though you've never a trinket left to give,
   You have nothing whatever to dread,
   For all I want is your firstborn child,
   If you and the King are wed."

"Perhaps it will never happen," thought the girl. "Perhaps he will forget. And if I refuse, I shall surely die." So she gave her word, and once more he spun and sang:

"A handful of straw and a whir, whir, whir,
   Knotweed, bindweed, and cockleburr.
   Three times round, and the job is done,
   The child is mine, and the gold is spun!"

When the King arrived at dawn, he gazed at the glittering room and shivered with joy. "We must be married, my dear," said he. "At once!" And so they were.

A year later a daughter was born, and the Queen loved her dearly. But one day, as she was playing with the girl, the door burst open and there stood the gnomish creature, smirking. He skipped right up to the child, poked at her, and chortled:

"Remember, Madam, you gave your word
A year ago this time;
You married the King, you bore a child—
And the child you bore is *mine*."

The terrified Queen offered him all the treasures of the kingdom if she could only keep her daughter, but he laughed and said:

"I can enter a twice-locked room,
Or turn a billygoat into a broom,
I can spin riches, silver and gold—
'Tis a living creature I long to hold."

The Queen was aghast. She trembled and wept so hopelessly, and clung to her little girl so desperately, that even the scoundrel's heart was softened. He cocked his ugly head, stared at her from under his bushy brows, and said:

> "A year spins by with a whir, whir, whir,
> Fireweed, bitter vetch, cockleburr.
> I give you three days to play my game:
> You may keep your child if you guess my name!"

The Queen lay awake all night, thinking of every name she had ever heard; and in the morning she sent a messenger out all over the land to discover even more. When the troublesome fellow appeared again, she tried them all. "Is it Caspar, Melchior, or Balthazar?" she inquired.

> "Is it Crumple or Blister, or Guggle or Nank?
> Williwaw, Flimflam, or Hiccup or Clank?"

But her visitor grinned from one crumpled ear to the other and said:

"You have not guessed my name.
Two days remain!"

On the second day, the Queen again sent her messenger out to inquire of all the neighbors the most curious names they knew, and when the rascal returned, she was ready for him.

"Is it Hailstone or Carbuncle, Jostle or Clench?
Millipede, Doldrum, Persnickety, Stench?"

But he shook his head with an impudent leer, and whooped:

"You have not guessed my name.
One day left of the game!"

On the third day, the Queen begged her messenger to ask at every remaining house, no matter how humble, and to bring her every name he could find, no matter how ridiculous. The man went out before dawn, and was back near midnight, and when he returned he said:

"Your Highness, not one new name could I find, though I searched from hither to thither, and on to yon. But when, at last, I reached the high mountain at the end of the deep forest, where the sun and the moon hold hands, I saw a little house with a bonfire burning before it. Around the fire a preposterous mite of a man was capering. He hopped and he leapt, and he sang at the top of his lungs:

'Vinegar, wormwood, gallstone, brine,
The child of the Queen will soon be mine.
Earthquake, firestorm, and hurricane,
Rumpelstiltskin is my name!'"

"It is indeed!" cried the Queen. And when that personage appeared, she had to cover her lips, for she could not keep from smiling.

"Well, now, Madam, the final test—
Give me my name, or the child at your breast!"

he demanded, with his fingers twitching, and his mean little eyes afire.

"Is it Chilblain or Earwig, or Dudgeon or Damp?
Is it Crumble or Fumble, or Lumpfish or Cramp?"

"That is not my name!
I have won the game!"

he shouted, and stretched out his hands for the babe.

"Not Foofuraw, Fistula, Fungus, or Wen?

———

Why—can it be RUMPELSTILTSKIN, then?"

crowed the Queen.

"Fire and brimstone! Ashes and bile!
The Devil told you, that old reptile!"

bawled the creature; and in his fury he stamped his right foot so hard that it sank down into the ground clear up to his hip, and stuck there.

"Rumpel and Pumpel and Stilt and Skin,
There's a hole in the ground and my leg's gone in.
I'll teach it a lesson, whatever I do,
I'll give it a terrible *Oo-Loo-Loo*,"

he thundered. And in a vengeful rage he pulled so ferociously at the leg that he ripped himself clean in two. So that was the end of him, at last.

Is it wicked to smile?
Well, the villain *was* vile.
And as for the King,
Rapacious old thing,
He got all the loot—
And a princess to boot!

Beauty and the Beast

There was once a wealthy merchant who lost his fortune and had to move from his big townhouse to a little cottage in the country. When he told his three daughters, the two older ones were furious. "What? Give up our parties and dances for a dismal cowpatch life?" they exclaimed. "Never!" They were sure that their lack of money would make no difference to their fashionable admirers, but they were quite mistaken. Their elegant friends laughed when they heard the news, and sang:

> "Let them prance through the fields
> In chiffon and high heels,
> Raising arrogant brows
> At the goggle-eyed cows!"

But they all felt sorry for the third daughter, who was so good and so lovely that she was called Beauty. Beauty didn't complain about leaving the city. "Never mind," she said to her father, "we'll make the best of it. Who knows, perhaps it will even suit us." And when the family had settled into their humble new home, she did all she could to make it a cheerful place. Her sisters treated her rudely and left the housework to her, while they sulked, slept late, and groaned about having nothing whatever to do and no one amusing to do it with.

After a year of rustic life, the father had to go on a journey, in hopes of regaining some of his wealth. "What shall I bring you from town?" he asked his daughters. "Fringed gowns and silk stockings!" exclaimed the older sisters, though they had no place to wear them. "Feathered hats! Kid gloves!"

But Beauty said, "There are no roses in our garden. I would love to have just one." She would not even have asked for that, but she didn't want her sisters to say she was trying to make them look greedy.

The merchant was badly cheated in town, and he had to return home poorer than before. The weather was bitter, he lost his way in the forest, and his horse slipped in the snow, throwing him to the ground. The poor man feared he would freeze to death or be eaten by the wolves he heard howling nearby. "I will never see my children again," he thought in despair. But then he caught sight of a light glowing through the trees. Hurrying toward it, he came to a splendid palace. His horse trotted after him, both of them starved and weary. There was not a soul to be seen, so the merchant led his horse to the stable and tethered it there. The famished animal attacked the oats and hay, while the man went on to the palace. He found himself in a great hall with a roaring fire and a table set before it laden with many sumptuous dishes. The merchant sat down to dry himself before the fire saying, "I hope whoever lives in this place won't think I am making myself too much at home." He waited for several hours, but no one came. Finally his hunger overwhelmed him, and he helped himself to a piece of roast chicken, devouring it gratefully and washing it down with two glasses of excellent wine. Dry and fed, he took courage and began to explore the castle. He walked through many magnificent rooms filled with costly furniture, carpets, and paintings. When he came to one with a fine big bed, he threw himself upon it and fell into a deep sleep.

He awoke at ten the next morning to find that handsome new clothes had replaced his torn and filthy ones. The snow had vanished and the sun shone on a garden filled with the most extraordinary flowers. In the great hall, a hearty breakfast was laid out for him. As he ate, he said aloud, "Thank you, good host, for this excellent breakfast, and for all your kindness."

When the merchant had downed his second cup of chocolate, he went to fetch his horse. Passing through the garden, he remembered Beauty's wish, took out his pocketknife, and cut a single red rose. No sooner had he done so than he heard a horrible noise, and a hideous beast appeared before him. "Ungrateful wretch," it roared, "I have saved your life, and you repay me by stealing the roses that are dearer to me than anything in the universe! For that, you shall die. I give you fifteen minutes in which to prepare yourself."

The poor merchant fell to his knees. "My Lord," he cried, "I never meant to rob you, I only wanted to bring a rose to my daughter."

"I am not a Lord," snarled the monster, "I am a Beast. Speak plainly, for flattery will not save you. You have a daughter?"

"Three," whispered the merchant.

"I shall spare you," the monster said, "but only if one of those daughters

consents to die in your place. Mind you, I won't have her unless she comes of her own free will. And you must return in three months if they all refuse."

"Never," the father thought, "would I sacrifice one of my children to this foul creature. But if I agree, I will be able to embrace them one last time before I die." And so he gave his word.

"Go," said the Beast. "And you shall not return home empty-handed. In the chamber where you slept, there is a chest. Fill it with anything you like, and I will send it after you." And the Beast departed. The father returned to his room and found the chest, as well as a quantity of thick gold pieces, which he packed into it. "At least I will leave my poor children something," he said.

He fetched his horse from the stable and set off, unable to see the way for his weeping. The horse found the road through the forest, and before long he was at the door of his little house. When his children ran to greet him, he held up the rose and said, "Here, my Beauty, I did not forget you. But I have paid a heavy price for this single blossom." And he told them his story.

The two eldest daughters began to wail and tear at their hair, and revile

Beauty for what she had brought upon them. "You couldn't have been satisfied with pretty clothes, or a little silver ring," they shrieked. "No, you were too proud. Now you will be the death of our poor dear father, and you can't be bothered even to shed a tear!"

"No need for that," replied Beauty. "He will not die, for I intend to go to the Beast myself." Her father would not hear of it, but Beauty could not be shaken. "It is all because of my rose," she said, and that was that.

When the father went to his room that night, he was astonished to find the chest full of gold, which he had forgotten in his sorrow. He did not tell his older daughters about it, for fear they would want to move right back to town and spend it all; but he did confide in Beauty. "While you were away," she said, "two gentlemen came who wanted to marry my sisters. If you give them the gold for their weddings, they will be happy, and you will be at peace."

When three months had passed, the father gave the gold to the delighted sisters and set off with Beauty for the palace. Her sisters were glad to see her go, but rubbed onions in their eyes to make themselves weep. The clever horse found his way in just a few hours. It trotted off on its own to the stable, where invisible hands made it comfortable, while the man and his daughter entered the palace. The great hall was all alight, the table was set with two places and covered with delicacies. The wretched father was too distraught to think of eating, but Beauty served him and made him taste each wonderful dish. She ate quite heartily, thinking, "If the Beast wants to fatten me up before he devours me, I might as well enjoy a good dinner myself."

No sooner had they finished than they heard a tremendous noise, and the Beast appeared. When she saw how repulsive he was, Beauty was aghast and could not keep herself from shuddering. But the Beast only asked her, "Have you come to me willingly, to die in place of your father?"

She could not speak, but managed to stammer, "Yes. Willingly."

"Your father," said he, "may stay this night. Then he must go and return no more." He bade them goodnight, and left them. They went to their rooms and slept, in spite of the grief in their hearts, and Beauty dreamed that a wise old woman came to her and said:

"Courage, Beauty, kind and true.
Your gifts shall be returned to you."

In the morning she told her father the dream, but he could not be comforted. "Ah, my poor child, that was only a dream," he said, "but this Beast is all too real." They put their arms around each other and wept bitterly. He left, and she was alone.

"If the Beast is going to eat me up tonight," said Beauty, drying her eyes, "why shouldn't I spend the afternoon exploring his palace?" She wandered in amazement from room to room, till she came to a door upon which was written, in letters of gold, BEAUTY'S APARTMENT. She opened it and found herself in an enchanting series of rooms, prettily furnished just to her liking and filled with books, music, even a harpsichord. "Well," she thought, "the Beast has gone to a good deal of trouble if he means to gobble me up in just a few hours. Perhaps there is hope for me yet." She picked up a book and, opening it, saw inscribed in golden letters:

Welcome, Beauty, claim thy place,
Dwell with happiness and grace.
At thy bidding, all shall be
Gladly given unto thee.

"This Beast," said she, "is not as savage as he seems." She spent the day pleasantly in her apartment, and in the evening went to the great hall, where music was playing, candles were lit, and the table was set for her supper.

As she seated herself, she heard the noise of the Beast, and she could not keep from trembling with fear when he entered. But all he said was "Do go on eating. I would only like to sit with you, if you will let me."

"Why, as you wish," replied Beauty.

"No," said he. "You are the mistress here, and if the sight of me offends you, I must leave. But tell me, Beauty, am I not extremely ugly?"

"You are," she said sorrowfully.

"And I am sometimes foolish, and never witty," he continued.

"If you were foolish, you would not know it," she said. "And truly, Beast, you are so gentle that I don't mind your frightful looks."

"Perhaps. But still, I *am* a Beast," he sighed. The monster sat quietly regarding her for a time, and then he asked, "Beauty, will you be my wife?" With that, all her terror came upon her again, and she sat speechless, afraid that if she refused he might murder her in his rage. But at last she answered, quaking, "No, Beast, I will not."

The room echoed with his terrible sighs and groans, but he got up and left her, saying, "Good night, Beauty."

"What a pity," she thought, "that such a gentle spirit should live in such a grotesque body."

For three months Beauty lived in the palace, content to read, listen to music, and walk in the wonderful gardens. The Beast came to sit with her as she ate her supper, and talked so good-naturedly that each evening as the hour drew near she began to look impatiently at the clock to see if he was late. But every visit ended with the same sad question: "Beauty, will you be my wife?"

And she was forced each time to answer, just as mournfully, "No, Beast. I will not." Till finally she said, "It pains me so that you force me to refuse you. You are my dearest friend—please try to be content with that."

"As I have no choice, I will," said he. "But I love you greatly, and I could not stand to lose you. Promise you will never leave me."

"I would promise gladly, Beast, but I miss my father so much. If I can't see him soon, I know I shall die of it."

"I would rather perish myself," said he, "than cause you any suffering. I will send you home, and it is your poor Beast who shall die of grief."

"No," said Beauty, in tears. "I couldn't bear to cause your death. Just let me stay one week with my father, and I swear I will return to you."

"You will be with him in the morning. But remember your promise, and when you are ready to come back to me put your ring on a table before you go to bed. Farewell, dear Beauty," and he left her, sighing his deep, windy sigh.

The next morning Beauty awoke in her father's house. The good merchant was overcome with joy to find her there, and hugged her for a long time.

Beside her bed stood a great jeweled trunk, overflowing with gowns embroidered in gold and diamonds. "You see," she exclaimed, "how thoughtful my good Beast is! I'll choose just one, and give the others to my sisters." But no sooner had the words left her lips than the trunk vanished.

"I believe the Beast must want you to keep them for yourself," her father said. And the trunk reappeared.

Beauty's sisters had married while she was gone, thanks to the gold the Beast had given their father. They came to pay her a visit, bringing their husbands. One was so much in love with himself that he couldn't be bothered to think of his wife at all; while the other had a mean, sharp tongue, which he used to mock and torment everyone. The sisters were eaten alive with envy to see Beauty in her fine clothes, and to hear her tell of her wonderful life with the Beast. They slipped away to the garden together, and soaked each other's shoulders with tears of rage at the thought of Beauty's happiness. "Why does that tiresome girl deserve such luck and we such misery?" the younger asked.

"It's unnatural!" cried the elder. "Suppose we keep her at home for more

than a week? Perhaps that precious monster of hers will fly into a rage and tear her to bits."

When the seventh day arrived, they sniveled and sobbed and pretended to be so miserable that Beauty could not endure it and let herself be persuaded to stay for another week. But her heart ached with the thought of the suffering she would cause the Beast, and she longed to see him again.

On the tenth night at her father's house, Beauty dreamed that she stood in the palace garden, weeping over the Beast, who lay dying on the grass. He gazed up at her sadly and gasped:

"What, faithless Beauty, come to say good-bye
And watch the foul Beast, broken-hearted, die?"

She awoke drenched in tears. "How could I have been so wicked?" she cried. "I have murdered my good, kind Beast, when I ought to have married him!" She jumped up, put her ring on the table, and went back to sleep at once.

When she awakened, she was at the Beast's palace again. Overjoyed, she put on the gown the Beast loved best, and waited the whole long day for him to find her. At last it was nine o'clock, but no Beast appeared. "I have killed him!" she cried, and ran desperately through the palace calling his name. Then she remembered her dream and flew to the garden. There he lay on the path, the poor Beast; he seemed to be dead. She threw herself down upon him and cried, "Oh, my beloved Beast, don't die!" And she felt a small beating of his heart. She raced to the well, drew up water, and sprinkled his face.

The Beast opened his eyes. "Beauty," he whispered, "you forgot your promise. I could not live with my grief and decided to starve myself to death. Now that I see you once more, I shall die happy."

"No, dearest Beast, you mustn't die, you must live to marry me, and we will never be parted again. I love you."

The moment she spoke those words the palace lit up, dazzling lights danced in the air, triumphant music rang out. When she turned back to the Beast, it was not a loathsome creature that lay at her feet but a handsome young prince.

"Thank you, dearest Beauty," he said tenderly, "for breaking the evil spell that bound me and restoring me to my true shape."

"But where is my Beast?" she cried, bereft.

"Here, here at your feet," said he. "A wicked fairy condemned me to a monster's form and deprived me of my wit, until a young woman should consent to marry me. You alone were able to see the goodness in my heart, and were generous enough to overlook my ugliness. Now I will ask you once again—Beauty, will you be my wife?"

"My own beloved Beast, my Prince, I will!" cried Beauty, and she gave him her hand. Together they returned to the castle, where her father was waiting, and her sisters, and the wise old woman she had seen in her dream.

"Beauty," said this woman:

"Now shall your sorrows all be left behind,
And you shall reign, a queen both just and kind.
But these two sisters, jealous, cold, and vain,

Must be condemned to suffer grievous pain.
As statues they shall stand, to guard your gate,
And witness all your joy, until their hate
Shall turn to shame, and they at last confess
Their malice, greed, and utter heartlessness."

Then, with a wave of her hand, the woman transported all of them to the kingdom of the Prince, where his subjects greeted him jubilantly. There Beauty and the Prince were married, and lived lovingly ever after.

And what more could you wish?
The moon on a dish?

Hansel and Gretel

In a wretched hut at the edge of a forest, Hansel and Gretel, too hungry to sleep, lay awake. On the other side of the flimsy wall, their parents were whispering. "What shall I do?" said the father, a poor woodcutter. "The cupboard is nearly empty. There is barely enough in the house to make a mouthful for two."

"We have two too many," their stepmother said. "We must save ourselves. We will take the children into the woods and *lose* them."

"My children?" exclaimed the father. "Never!"

"Tomorrow," said his wife. And though at first he refused, she kept at him until he agreed.

Gretel wept into her little straw pillow, but her brother opened the door and crept out into the moonlight. He stuffed his pockets with small white pebbles that glittered like teeth.

In the morning the stepmother shook them awake. "Stir your bones," said she. "We're off to the forest to gather wood, and we've no time to waste on idlers. Here is some bread for your dinner. If you are smart, you'll save it up, for it's all you will get." And she gave them two dry crusts, which Gretel put in her apron pocket.

As they walked along, Hansel kept stopping and glancing back at the hut. "Come ahead, lazy legs. Why are you dawdling?" asked his father.

"I'm just waving good-bye to my little white cat, up there on the roof," said Hansel, who was really stopping each time to throw one of the white stones over his shoulder onto the path.

"The lumpish clodpate, he can't tell a cat from a beam of sun on the chimney," scolded the stepmother.

When they had gone very deep into the forest, the father said to them, "Gather some wood, and I will make you a good cheerful fire." So the children gathered a huge pile of brushwood, and their father lit it. When it had blazed up high, the stepmother said sweetly, "Now, children, have your dinner and lie down to rest by the fire, while we chop wood in the forest. Then we'll come back to fetch you." The children did as they were told, hoping their parents would not abandon them after all. At noon, they nibbled their bit of

bread, and listened for the sound of their father's axe, but they heard nothing. At last they grew weary with waiting and fell into a deep sleep. When they awoke, it was night, and they were still alone.

"They're not coming back, are they?" said Gretel.

"No, Gretel," said Hansel, "they won't be back. But look, the moon is shining on my path of white pebbles, and it will lead us home."

As the sun was rising, they knocked at the door of their hut, and their father was overjoyed to see them. He had been weeping over the loss of his children, sure that the wild beasts must have torn them to bits. But the stepmother scowled, and said, "What wicked children you are, to sleep so long in the woods, and frighten your poor parents nearly to death."

A few nights later, the woman whispered again to her husband. "Soon we shall have nothing to eat but the dishes themselves. The children must go." The father resisted, but the woman would not relent, so it was agreed.

The children heard everything. Hansel wanted to go out and collect his pebbles, but this time he found the door locked. "Don't be afraid," he said to his sister, "we'll find a way."

The next morning, just as before, the woman gave them two small crusts of bread, and they all set off for the woods. Again Hansel kept turning back toward the hut, and his father scolded him, "Move along, scatterbrain. Can't you just walk in a straight line for once?"

"Yes, Father, but I must wave goodbye to my little white dove up there on the roof," said Hansel, who was really throwing the crumbs of his bread on the path behind him.

"Oh, the hopeless ninny! He can't tell a dove from a sunbeam," the stepmother jeered.

They walked even further than they had the first time; and by and by they came to a part of the wood the children had never seen. Again they were told to gather brushwood for a fire, and to wait beside it until their parents returned. Gretel shared her little crust with Hansel, and they fell asleep. When the moon awakened them, Hansel looked for his trail of crumbs, but hungry birds had eaten them, and the children were left to wander, lost, in the dark wood. For three days and three nights they strayed, with nothing to eat but a few bitter berries, and no bed but the cold hard ground. "We shall starve," they said. "We shall die." And they sat down under a tree and cried together.

At noon that day a beautiful snow-white bird began to sing above them so marvelously that the children quite forgot their grief. When its song was finished, the bird flew off, and they followed it deeper and deeper into the wood. At last it came to a little house and alit on the roof. When Hansel and Gretel drew near, they saw that the house was made of gingerbread and was covered all over with tiny cakes. Its windows were clear sugar that gleamed in the sun. The famished children fell upon it. Hansel chewed up a piece of the roof, while Gretel munched on a bit of window. As they ate, they heard a soft voice inside, singing:

"Gnaw, nibble, crunch! Can it be a mouse
That feasts on the roof of my poor little house?"

The children were unperturbed. They tore off great chunks of roof and a whole windowpane, and with their mouths full, sang:

> "It is only the wind, and never a mouse,
> That nibbles and gnaws on your sweet little house."

All at once the door burst open and out flew a hag as twisted and dry as an old boot. Hansel and Gretel were frightened out of their wits, and clung together, but the old woman spoke kindly to them and invited them in with a tender little song:

> "Welcome, dear children, come in and find rest—
> I'll take care of you both, in the way I know best."

And she sat them down at a table full of enchanting dishes they'd never tasted before. When they had finally eaten and drunk their fill, she led them to two little beds, with sheets as soft as a spider's web, and Hansel and Gretel fell fast

asleep, believing themselves in the house of a good angel.

But the old crone was really an evil witch who had built her gingerbread house just in order to lure little children into her clutches, so that she could cook them and eat them. Though she could not see very far with her weak red eyes, her nose always told her when human children were near, and she had been waiting eagerly for Hansel and Gretel. The next morning she sniffed greedily at the sleeping pair, smacked her dry lips, and said to herself:

"What a savory supper these two will provide!
But they must be fattened before they are fried."

And she snatched Hansel out of his bed with her bony hand, carried him off to a cage, and locked him up. He shouted and flung himself at the bars, but it did him no good, for the witch had no mercy in her. She returned to her house and shook Gretel awake, saying:

"Up, sluggard! Start cooking a rich fricassee
To fatten your brother, my supper-to-be.
I'll roast him with rosemary! What a delight
To relish each sizzling, succulent bite."

Though Gretel wept and pleaded, it was no use. The old witch grinned, and forced the girl to obey. Each day all sorts of delectable dishes were cooked for Hansel, but Gretel was given nothing but crab shells to eat. Each morning the harpy went to the cage and commanded, "Hansel, Hansel, put out your thumb," for she wanted to see if he was fat enough. But Hansel stuck out a little bone, and the witch, who was nearly blind, felt it and was amazed that, however much he was fed, he remained so thin. After a month had gone by, her stomach began to rumble and roar, and she couldn't wait any longer.

"Hansel skinny or Hansel fat,
He shall be eaten, and that is that,"

she croaked gleefully. Gretel cried till her eyes swelled shut, but the witch had no heart in her bony chest, only a great hunger.

Early next morning the merciless creature forced Gretel outside to light a fire and hang up a cauldron of water.

"I will have bread with my Hansel feast.
The dough has risen, the pan is greased,"

said she, and catching Gretel by her hair, she hauled her over to the oven, in which flames leapt and coals hissed.

"Go try out the oven, the coals are red.
Is it hot enough yet to bake my bread?"

she snarled. She thought she might as well have the two at once and make a banquet of it. But Gretel understood what the hag was after, and answered:

"Pardon me, Mistress, the door is so small,
I could never squeeze into the oven at all."

At that, the hag shook her fists and shouted:

"You nincompoop, you're as thin as a gnat.
I could squeeze in myself, and I'm twice as fat!"

And to prove it, she popped her head in the oven.

Then Gretel gave her a tremendous shove and into the oven she flew, and bang went the door behind her. Gretel fastened the iron bolt and covered her ears, so as not to hear the horrible shrieks and howls of the evil old hag as she burnt to a handful of cinders. Gretel ran to the cage where Hansel sat. "We're free," she cried, as she undid the lock, "we're free, and nothing remains of that horrid old witch but ashes!"

The children embraced each other, and then ran shouting and singing into

the witch's house, where there was nothing left to fear. They found it was crowded in every corner with chests full of silver and pearls and precious stones of all colors and shapes.

"These are certainly better than pebbles or crumbs!" cried Hansel.

He filled up his pockets, and Gretel filled hers as well. "I believe it's time to go home," she said. With that, they ran out of the witch's house and into the wood. For two hours they walked, until they arrived at a wide, wide river, and there they stopped, for there was no way across it. In the middle, a little white duck was diving and splashing, with not a care in the world. Gretel called out to it:

"Sweet bird, kind bird, good-luck-giver,
Ferry two children over the river."

The little duck came to them at once, and Hansel jumped on her back.

"Come on, Gretel," cried he, but Gretel saw that the two of them would make too heavy a burden.

"No, Hansel, we must go one at a time," she said. So the duck took Hansel across and then went back for Gretel. They thanked her well and walked straight on into the wood, which did not seem so strange or so dark as it had on the other side. Before very long, they spied their house and ran through the door, right into their father's arms.

"My children, my dear ones!" he cried, and hugged them tenderly. He had grieved so long that he'd filled both a barrel and a bucket with his tears. "You're home, and you've nothing to fear anymore, for my wife, that wicked woman, is dead."

"And so is the bad old witch!" cried Gretel, and she began to throw handfuls of precious jewels into her father's lap. Hansel joined in, flinging pieces of glittering silver into the air. There was no limit to their rejoicing.

Their troubles were ended.
Life was splendid!

Little Red Riding Hood

The two things your grandmother loves best in this world are you and custard pie," said Little Red Riding Hood's mother. "She's been sick, so I've made a custard pie for you to bring her."

"I will," said Little Red Riding Hood.

"Stay on the path, keep your wits about you, say good morning nicely, and don't go snooping into every corner," said her mother.

"I will, I will, I will, and I won't," promised Little Red Riding Hood, pulling on the red cloak her grandmother had made for her, and slinging the basket of pie over her arm.

She had not gone far on her way through the woods when a great gray wolf strolled out of the shadowy trees and into her path. "Good morning, my sweet," he cooed.

"And good morning to you," replied Little Red Riding Hood, who had never before laid eyes on a wolf and had no idea how evil a creature he was.

"Where are you off to, so bright and early, and what do you have in that pretty basket?" inquired the wolf, sniffing it hopefully.

"I'm off to visit my grandmother, with a custard pie," said she.

"Yum," said the wolf. But he was licking his chops over Little Red Riding Hood, not the pie. "What an exquisite dinner she'd make, so toothsome and tender," he said to himself. "As for the grandmother—tough and stringy, no doubt. But then, why shouldn't I dine on them both—with custard pie for dessert!" He did not dare attack Little Red Riding Hood on the spot, because a woodsman was chopping trees nearby, and the wolf was afraid of his axe. So he sauntered along beside her, switching his tail in anticipation.

By and by, the wolf asked, "Have you far to go?"

"My grandmother's house is just beyond the old mill, under the three big oak trees, sir," replied Little Red Riding Hood. "There's something about him I don't quite care for," she thought, "but I'm not supposed to be rude."

"Ah, yes, I know the place," said the wolf. "You'll be there before noon. But see here, my girl. Violets are blooming, finches are singing, the sun is tickling the little green leaves, and here you are, tramping along as if you were late for school. Why don't you look around you a bit, and enjoy the world?"

"What a good idea," she exclaimed, pushing her hood back and gazing about at the bright spring flowers blossoming all around her. "I believe I shall pick a fine bouquet for my poor sick Granny!" And she skipped off the path and began at once. But for every flower she chose there was another even more beautiful farther on, and so she strayed deeper and deeper into the woods, and out of her way.

"Ta-ta!" the wolf called after her, and he trotted straight off to the grandmother's house, where he knocked at the door.

"Who's there?" called the grandmother, in a quavery voice.

"It's your Little Red Riding Hood, with a custard pie from Mama," called the wolf, in as high a voice as he could manage.

"Lift up the latch, my dear, and open the door," answered the grandmother. "I am still too weak to get out of bed." The wolf did as she said, and when he had the door open, he bounded into the house and gobbled the poor old woman up before she had time to sneeze. He shut the door, dressed himself in a night-gown he took from the cupboard, and put on her pretty lace cap. Then he leapt into her bed and pulled the curtains close around him.

By and by, Little Red Riding Hood arrived and knocked at the door. "Who's there?" called the wolf, in as quavery a voice as he could manage.

"Little Red Riding Hood, with a custard pie," called the child.

"Lift up the latch, my precious, and open the door," croaked the wolf.

"Poor Granny is certainly hoarse today," thought Little Red Riding Hood. "I've a strange sort of stay-away feeling, I don't know why." Nevertheless, she lifted the latch and entered. "Good morning, Granny," she called, glancing about. There was no answer, so she went to the bed and opened the curtains. There lay Granny, her cap pulled down, not looking herself at all. "My, my, Granny, what big furry ears you have!" cried Little Red Riding Hood.

"The better to hear you with, my pet," breathed the wolf.

"Dear me, Granny, what enormous eyes you have!"

"The better to see you with, my sweet."

"And good gracious, Granny, what huge hairy arms you have!"

"The better to hug you with, my dear."

"Oh, heavens, Granny, what terrible long sharp teeth you have!"

"The better to eat you with!" cried the wolf, and he jumped up and swallowed Little Red Riding Hood in one single gulp. Then he lay down in the old lady's bed and, being so stuffed, fell sound asleep and began to snore.

A huntsman was passing the door at that very moment, and he said to himself, "The old woman is snorting like a hog, perhaps she's come down sick again," and he hurried into the house. When he saw the wolf asleep in the grandmother's cap, he fell into a rage and lifted his gun to shoot the beast. "Whoa, not so fast!" he said to himself. "That old woman has got to be someplace, and there seems to be only one place she could be." With that, he took up a scissors and snipped a good-sized slit in the sleeping wolf's stomach.

"Oh, do let me out!" gasped Little Red Riding Hood. "It's hot and it's dark and it smells like rotten eggs!" And out she jumped.

"Oh, do let me out!" wheezed Granny. "I've a crick in my neck and a stitch in my side and a cramp in both of my legs!" And out she clambered, stiff and sore. Then Little Red Riding Hood ran outside and collected an armful of huge heavy stones, which they stuffed into the belly of the sleeping wolf; and Granny took her needle and sewed him up neatly. When she cut the thread, the wolf awoke, and seeing his dinner standing before him, he wanted to run away. But the stones in his belly were too heavy, and at the first step he collapsed and fell right down dead. Then Little Red Riding Hood, her grandmother, and the hunter sat down and refreshed themselves nicely with the custard pie, which the wolf had forgotten to eat.

Wasn't that fun?
Now the tale is done.

The Frog Prince

Along time ago, when magic was more of an everyday matter, a certain young princess was in the habit of wandering into the woods near her father's palace. She liked to sit by the side of a cool spring, in the shade of an old lime tree, and play with a little golden ball which she always carried in her pocket.

One dull afternoon the Princess was amusing herself in her usual way, throwing her ball up into the air and catching it, when she threw it so high that it bounced onto the grass and rolled right into the spring. She peered down after it, but her ball had vanished, and she could see nothing but her own astonished face. "Oh, my precious golden ball! I would give all I have for my pretty gold ball!" she wailed. "How shall I ever manage to live without it?" And as her cries and lamentations grew louder and louder, a frog poked his big ugly head up out of the water and asked:

"Why do you weep so, King's young daughter?
Your tears are bitter, they trouble the water."

"Go away, you web-footed thing," she sobbed. "Can't you see that I'm crying for my golden ball, which has fallen into the spring and is lost forever?"

"Hi-ho," croaked the frog.

> "Forever is much too long a time
> For gold to lie covered in muck and slime.
> What would you give me if I should fetch,
> This instant, your beautiful Throw-and-Catch?"

"I'll give you whatever you like, dearest frog," said the Princess. "For instance, my amethyst beads, my mauve silk dress with lace at the neck, and even my golden crown."

> "Though I'm sure I'd look elegant, there in the weeds,
> With my fine silken dress and my amethyst beads,
> Not to mention those webs which, connecting my toes,

Have provoked you to wrinkle your ravishing nose,
And my huge warty head, in its circlet of gold,
I would rather, my dear, if I might be so bold,
Remain as I am for the moment. If you
Will but grant me your friendship, and cherish me true,
And allow me to dine from your dainty gold dish
(I am partial to gnats, but I never touch fish),
If you'll carry me up to your pretty white bed,
And pillow me next to your exquisite head,
Then I'll dive to the depths of the spring and retrieve
The trinket for which you incessantly grieve,"

answered the frog, gazing at her with his great bulging eyes.

"Oh, yes," said the Princess, drying her tears, "I'll be delighted to promise you all that you ask. Just bring me my dear little ball." But to herself she said, "Flumdiddle! This slimy creature belongs in the stream, and that's where he's going to stay."

Then the frog kicked up his heels, plunged down deep in the water, and in no time at all popped up with the ball in his mouth. With a twist of his head, he flung it out onto the grass, where the delighted Princess snatched it and dashed off, lickety-split, for the castle. The horrified frog hopped up onto the bank, stared after the girl, and croaked:

"Wait, wait, dear Princess, my legs are short.
It's a long, weary way from the stream to the court!"

But the Princess was gone, with not a thought in her head for the frog, who sank down sadly into the dark water.

That evening, just as the Princess, her father, and all his courtiers were sitting down to supper, they heard a strange sound and paused with their forks in the air to listen: *splish-splash, squish-squash*, something was making its way

very slowly up the great marble staircase. At last, with a final, determined *splat,* he arrived at the dining-hall door, tapped gently upon it, *pit-pit,* and cried in a small voice:

"Come to me, Princess, open the door.
I'm winded and worn and my bones are sore."

The Princess ran to the door to see who was calling, and when she opened it, there was the frog, squatting expectantly at her feet. She slammed the door as hard as she could and ran back to her chair with her face ablaze and her heart pounding.

The King saw how frightened she looked, and said, "What's this, daughter? Has a giant come to steal you away?"

"No," she said, "nothing like that. It's only a disgusting frog."

"And what," asked the King, "might a frog want with a princess?"

"Oh, Father, this morning the golden ball you gave me fell into the spring, and I cried so hard that this frog heard me and brought it back. But before he would do it, the nasty creature forced me to promise that he could be my friend, and eat from my plate, and even sleep next to me in my bed. I didn't believe he would ever escape from the spring, but now here he is at the door, and he wants to come in!"

The frog tapped again, *pit-pit*, and said:

> "Open the door, your love has come.
> Why do you sit so cold and dumb?
> Oh, what of the vows that you made to me
> In the noonday heat, by the old lime tree?"

Then the King said, "What you have promised, so you must do. Go at once and let him in."

So the Princess flung open the door, and the frog hopped in and followed her to the table, saying:

"Have you forgotten so soon, so soon,
The promise you made this afternoon?
Princess, why do you hesitate?
Come, let me dine from your golden plate."

The Princess recoiled, but her Father commanded her to do it; so she lifted the frog between two fingers and put him next to her plate. She came close to choking on every bite she took, but while the King and all his courtiers stared, the frog enjoyed himself immensely. When he had made a good meal of it, he said:

"Now carry me up to your clean white bed.
Let me share the pillow beneath your head."

The Princess sobbed, and ranted, and swore she would die if she had to touch the cold, clammy frog again. But her Father glared at her ferociously and said, "He was good enough for you when you needed him, and you've no right to look down on him now. Do as you promised." So she took the creature in her hand for the second time and carried him upstairs. When she reached her room, she set him down in the farthest, darkest corner, and crept shuddering into her bed. But the frog hopped over to her and said:

"Princess, my dear,
I shall never sleep there."

"Indeed, you will," said she. But he replied:

"I'll do no such thing.
I shall tell the King."

This infuriated the Princess so much that she snatched up the frog and hurled him against the wall with all her might, crying, "Now will you be quiet, you loathsome frog?" But even as he fell, he was transformed into a handsome

young Prince, with beautiful green eyes.

"Please don't be alarmed, my dearest," he said. "I was bewitched by an evil fairy and could not be restored to my true shape till a princess took me three times into her hand. Now the enchantment is broken, and if you will come with me to my kingdom and be my bride and Queen, we will be sure to live happily ever after."

The Princess was so delighted with her Prince that she accepted at once. Then she took him by the hand, kissed him, and led him straight downstairs to meet her father, who was only too pleased to give his consent to her marriage and immediate departure.

The next morning a carriage drove up, with eight fine horses, each wearing a white ostrich plume and a golden harness. Behind the carriage rode the young Prince's servant, Faithful Henry. This Henry had grieved so bitterly when his master was transformed that he had to bind up his chest with three iron bands, in order to keep his heart from bursting with sorrow. The Prince and Princess set off together, and along the way they were startled by three loud cracking sounds. The Prince turned and called, "Henry, Henry, the carriage is breaking!"

But Faithful Henry replied, "No, Master, it's only the bands on my chest, which are breaking for joy."

When they arrived at the Prince's kingdom, they were greeted by one hundred drums, one hundred trumpets, and a chorus of one hundred little boys and girls, all dressed in pink velvet with purple bows and sashes. The Prince and the Princess were married at once, on the balcony of the palace, so all their delighted subjects could enjoy the spectacle.

And was the Princess kind to her Prince?
Who knows? They have never been heard of since.

Jack and the Beanstalk

Long ago, in a faraway country, there lived a poor widow and her only son, Jack. Jack was lazy, it's true, and a bit foolish, but he was a good-hearted boy, and he loved his mother. The two of them had only their small cottage, with its dab of a garden, and an old cow called Blizzard, because she was as white as the milk she gave, except for a few spots to make her more interesting. Each morning they milked their cow and each afternoon they carried the milk to the market. It was all the income they had, and even so they lived on scraps and snippets.

One day when Jack's mother went out to milk Blizzard, there wasn't a drop to be got from her. "Oh, Jack, I'm afraid the poor old cow's gone dry!" said she, and they both stood sadly and gazed at Blizzard, who stared back sadly at them. "It can't be helped," said the mother. "She must be sold."

"Sell Blizzard?" said Jack.

"We can't feed ourselves, and we can't feed the cow," said his mother. "Of course, you *might* get a job."

"I doubt it," said Jack.

"Well then, you must take her to market and get as much as you can."

"I will,"said Jack. "I feel lucky today." And he took the cow by her halter and started off down the road. He hadn't gone far, just around two bends and a rather long curve, when he met a peculiar-looking old fellow.

"Good morning, Jack," said he, with an ear-to-ear smile.

"Good morning, indeed!" said Jack, amazed to hear his name on the lips of the strange fellow.

"And tell me then, Jack, where might you be going, with that amazingly white, spotted cow on the end of a string?"

"I am taking her off to the market to sell," replied Jack, "and I know I'm going to do well, because I feel lucky today."

"And you look lucky, too," said the man. "Here's a test for you: What's the difference between a bean and a billygoat?"

"Beans," replied Jack, "are much more agreeable."

"Oh, you're a shrewd boy, you'll go far," cried the man. "Look here, could these be the beans you had in mind?" And he reached into his pocket and pulled out a handful of weird-looking beans.

"I dunno," said Jack.

"Of course you don't," said the man, "you never saw anything like these beans in your life. And I'll tell you what. Since this is your lucky day, I believe I'll have to trade you my beans for that cow."

"Do I look that stupid?" asked Jack.

"Not you, nor your cow neither," the man replied. "And when I tell you the truth about these beans, you'll know you've managed to get the best of me. These remarkable beans, if planted tonight, will grow on up to the sky by morning. *Clear on up to the top of the sky.*"

"No fooling?" asked Jack. "I'd never have known it."

"You wheedled it out of me," the man said, frowning.

"The cow for the beans," cried Jack. "Agreed!"

"You drive a hard bargain," the man said. "But if you're dissatisfied, I'll give your old dry cow back—and you can keep the beans, too!" So saying, he placed the beans in Jack's hand and was off down the road, singing:

"I've got a cow, and her name is Blizz,
        She's a mighty fine cow, that's what she is!"

And Blizzard seemed to dance a little as they went along together.

Jack ran home to show his mother how shrewd a bargain he'd made. "I've sold her!" he cried, as he came through the door without wiping his feet.

"Good boy," said his mother. "And back so soon! How much did you get for her, Jack?"

"I'll give you a guess," said he.

"Five bits of silver? Ten? Fifteen?"

"Your boy's no fool," said he. "What's silver compared to a handful of guaranteed magical beans!"

"Beans?" cried his mother. "You've traded my Blizzard for beans? I'll bean you, you dolt, you ninny, you knucklehead! Here's what I think of your beans, you Jackanapes!" And she flung them out the window and burst into tears. There was nothing at all by way of supper for Jack, and he went upstairs

to bed feeling hungry and angry and sorry and sad. To make matters worse, he knew his poor mother was feeling the same.

Jack woke up early, knowing that something was not quite right, for the room was too dark. The window was shaded by an enormous beanstalk, sprung from the beans his mother had thrown away. It was twisted and thick, and it reached right up to the sky. "So there!" said Jack. He flung open the window, jumped onto the beanstalk, threw back his head, and began to climb. He climbed and he climbed and he climbed some more, and he kept on climbing till his head poked up through the highest clouds, and he stepped off into the sky.

Before him a long road stretched out straight, and he walked along it a long, long time, till at last he came to a house so huge that he felt like a cricket before it. A gigantic woman stood in the door. "Good morning, Madam," said Jack, whose mother had taught him manners. "I wonder if I could trouble you for a bit of breakfast. I had nothing at all to eat last night, or this morning, either, and I've had a good long climb."

"The trouble will all be yours," said she, "for my husband is bigger than

I am, and his favorite breakfast is little boys, fried crisp and served with hot-pepper sauce. Just hop along quick. He'll be home and hungry before you know it, and so much the worse for you."

"I haven't even the strength to crawl," said Jack, "without just a bite for my rumbling belly—I'll bet you can hear it."

"Well, come along in," said the giant's wife, "and take your chances." She wasn't so awful after all, and she sat Jack down to a plateful of bread and cheese, with a glass of milk besides.

"This is more like it," said Jack. He was just about to ask for seconds when the whole house began to rattle and shake, and so did he.

"There's my husband, I know his step," the giantess said. "Now what shall we do about you?"

"I dunno," said Jack.

"Come quick," she whispered, "and jump in the oven."

Jack lost no time in doing that, and a good thing, too, for the door flew open and in stumped the giant, roaring:

"Wife, Wife, what do I smell?
Tell me no tales, for my nose knows well.
Fee-Fi-Fo-Fum,
I smell the blood of an Englishman.
Be he alive, or be he dead,
I'll grind his bones to make my bread."

And he pounded his tremendous, mud-covered feet on the floor.

"Rubbish," said his wife, "your nose is having some fun with you. What it smells is rhinoceros ragout, which I'll serve up as soon as you've combed your hair and washed your hands, and not one minute before."

While Jack watched in horror through a chink in the oven, the giant combed his hair, washed his enormous hands, and sat down to devour the vast bowl of steaming meat that the giantess put before him. Though it seemed to Jack he would go on eating forever, at last he was done, and announced his satisfaction with a belch like the crack of doom. Then he called out:

"My bowl is empty, I've eaten the lot.
Now let me see how much treasure I've got."

His wife brought him three great sacks of gold from a chest in the corner and went off to take her nap. The giant began counting, but it wasn't long till his eyes closed and he fell asleep with his head on the table, snoring enough to wake the Devil.

Jack eased open the oven door and popped out ever so quietly. "I'll just take a lick of dessert," he said to himself, and snatched up a sack of gold. Then he flew out the door and headed straight for the beanstalk. When he reached it, he threw down the sack and scrambled after it, right into his mother's garden. And there she stood, poor woman, gazing up at the beanstalk and wondering where her foolish boy had gone, and where the sack had come from. When Jack showed her the gold, she was overjoyed and had to admit that the beans were magical after all.

"This will last us forever," said she.

"And a half," said Jack. Indeed, they did live well for a year, but then all the gold was spent. "Now what shall we do?" asked Jack's mother. "I'm afraid you will have to get yourself a job."

"Never mind," replied Jack, "there's more where that came from. I'll just have another bit of a climb." His mother begged him not to go, but it was no use. Up he went to the top of the beanstalk, and he skipped along till he came once more to the giant's house. There on the front step stood the giantess.

"Good morning, Madam," said Jack politely. "You see before you a dreadfully hungry boy."

"What of it?" said she.

"I had the idea you might be so kind as to lend me a speck of breakfast," said he.

"Go away," said she. "The only thing a boy will get here is eaten—except, that is, for the one last year, who looked rather like you, but skinnier. He escaped with a sack of gold, which made my husband extremely hard to live with, I'll tell you."

"My sympathy, Ma'am," said Jack, "and the breakfast needn't be anything fancy."

"You're a sweet talker," said the woman. "I'll let you come in, but I can't promise you won't be dessert for my husband."

"We'll just see who gets the dessert," said Jack to himself.

The giantess dished up a savory plateful of bread and cheese, which Jack ate with gusto. He was settling down for a nice little chat with the giantess, but then the giant's footsteps thundered, the walls shook, and Jack dived into the oven. The giant began his Fee-ing and Fi-ing and Fo-ing and Fum-ming again, and again his wife assured him that there was no English blood to be smelled. "It's only the buffalo bisque on the stove," said she. So the giant combed his hair, washed his hands, and sat down to stuff himself. Then he licked the bowl, belched mightily, and roared out:

"Wife, Wife, get up on your legs.
Bring me the hen that lays golden eggs."

"The gentleman calls for his golden eggs, tra-la," grumbled the giantess. Nevertheless, she went and fetched a little brown hen, set it on the table in front of her husband, and stalked off for her nap. "Lay!" commanded the giant, and the little hen cackled and laid a golden egg. "Again," he said, so she did it again, and a third time, too. The giant soon wearied of the game, put down his head, and fell to snoring. Out jumped Jack from the oven, scooped up the hen, and made for the door. But the startled hen let out a great cackle and the giant awoke. Then Jack lit out at a run down the road, with the giant raging and shouting:

"Where in the sky is my little brown hen?
Someone has been here thieving again!"

In fact, the hen was tucked snugly under Jack's arm as he streaked down the beanstalk and home to his mother's house, where he found her peering up, as if she were hoping to catch a glimpse of her son in the sky.

"Look, Ma!"cried he, setting the hen on the kitchen table. "Lay," he ordered. "Now lay again." And soon the table was covered with golden eggs.

Mother and son had an easy life, selling the eggs the little brown hen laid, one on weekdays and two on Sundays.

But by and by Jack became restless, for the giant's house had got into his head and seemed to be calling him. "Well, I'll just have one more visit upstairs," he said to himself. And early one morning before his mother awoke, he was off up the beanstalk again. He was afraid to try his luck with the giantess a third time, so he sneaked around the corner of the house and hid himself in a great copper pot that stood outside. Before very long the giant's footsteps drew near and made the pot ring so loudly that Jack was nearly deafened. The giant went into his house and bellowed:

"Fee-Fi-Fo-Fum,
I smell the blood of an Englishman.
I smell it loud, and I smell it clear.
I'm telling you, Wife, there's a young lad here!"

"Well, if there is, it's surely that sweet-talking scamp who stole your gold and your little brown hen. I'll bet he's weaseled his way back into my oven." They banged their heads together, trying to beat each other to the oven door, but of course there was nothing inside but a few old bones, and the giantess cried, "Oh, fie on your Fee-Fi-Fo-Fum, I'm sick of it. What you smell is boy, all right, but it's last night's leftover boy, that I've just warmed up for breakfast. Go wash your hands and comb your hair, and you'd better give your big stupid nose a good blow while you're at it."

So the giant sat down and ate his meal, and picked his teeth with the bones, while the giantess sat on the huge front step, right next to the pot with Jack inside, and muttered, "I yearn for a quiet life." Soon enough her husband belched and shouted:

"Wife, Wife, you'd better look sharp.
I'm in the mood for my golden harp."

The woman sighed, hauled herself up, and went into the house to hand him a harp of gold. Then she went off to bed. "Harp, play," said the giant, and the golden harp played a pavane. "Something livelier," ordered the giant. It played a little gavotte. "Let's have a lullaby," yawned the giant, and the golden harp played the sweetest lullaby any child could wish for. The giant's head hit the table with a thump, and his snores set Jack's copper pot a-rattle.

At that, Jack pushed up the lid and stole out, and into the house he crept, right up to the table. There he grabbed hold of the harp and made a leap for the door. But the harp had a voice of its own and cried out loudly, "Master, Master!" The giant awoke with a snort and gasped at the sight of Jack hot-footing it down the road with the harp in his hands. The giant lurched to his feet and bellowed:

"Stop, you scoundrel, you lummox, you flea,
I'll skin you alive with a Fo-Fum-Fee.
I'll smash you to smithers, I'll sliver your bones,
And I'll grind them up well for my muffins and scones!"

And out he dashed down the road after Jack. Jack had the head start, and fear enlivened his legs. He managed to reach the beanstalk ten leaps and a bound ahead of the giant's outstretched hand, and down he scrambled, as fast as he could, with the giant roaring behind him:

"You stole my treasure, my harp, and my hen,
But you'll never, no NEVER, come thieving again!"

What a commotion! The beanstalk shook with the giant's weight, Jack's teeth clattered with terror, the giant howled, and the magic harp played a wild mazurka. When he could see his house and yard below him, Jack called out, "Mother, hurry, bring me the axe!" Out rushed his mother with the axe in one hand and the dishrag in the other, crying, "Jack, oh, Jack, what can it be now?"

Jack jumped down, grabbed the axe, and chopped the beanstalk halfway through with one blow. As the giant's giant feet appeared above his head, Jack, exhausted, found the strength for a second great blow. The severed beanstalk crashed to the ground, and the giant pitched headfirst after it. And there he lay dead, with his Fe-Fi-Fo-Fum silenced forever. The harp played a dirge in his honor, then switched to a jolly tune for Jack and his mother.

So they had the golden harp for their pleasure and the little brown hen's eggs to keep them. Indeed, they were kept so very well that Jack never did have to do an honest day's work in his life. And as he was such a sweet-talking lad, he found himself a fine princess to marry, and they all got along quite nicely together as long as they lived.

And whatever became of the giant's wife?
Well, I guess she was granted her peaceful life.